Bernard makes a splash!

lisa stickley

There's a swimming pool contest that's held every year,
with a springboard SO tall that crowds gather and cheer.

The greatest thrill seekers
you ever did see,
these high diving dogs

(and
the
odd
swimming
flea).

Meet Bernard, our super shy high diving hound,
(confidence is something he's never quite found).

He wanted to dive, to perform his best jump,
but his knees started knocking, his heart went thump-thump!

He'd been pool manager for five years and two weeks.

Observing the divers, learning their techniques.

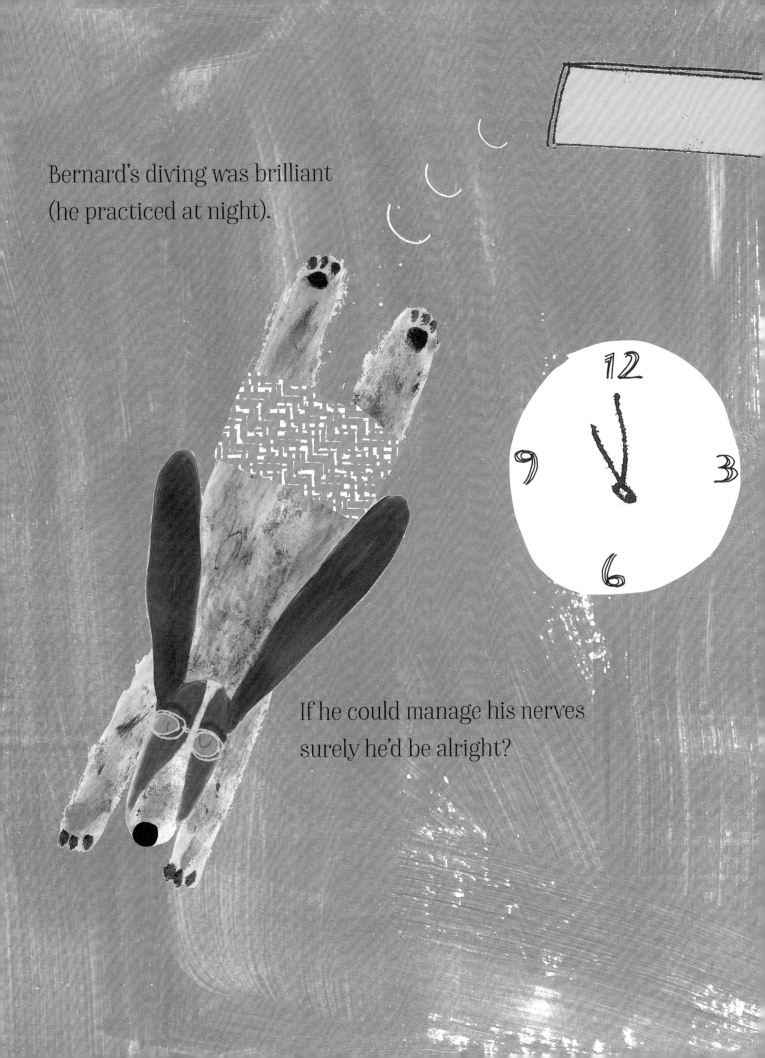

Bernard's diving was brilliant
(he practiced at night).

If he could manage his nerves
surely he'd be alright?

With a few days to go the contestants flew in,
from all over the world; each one hoping to win.

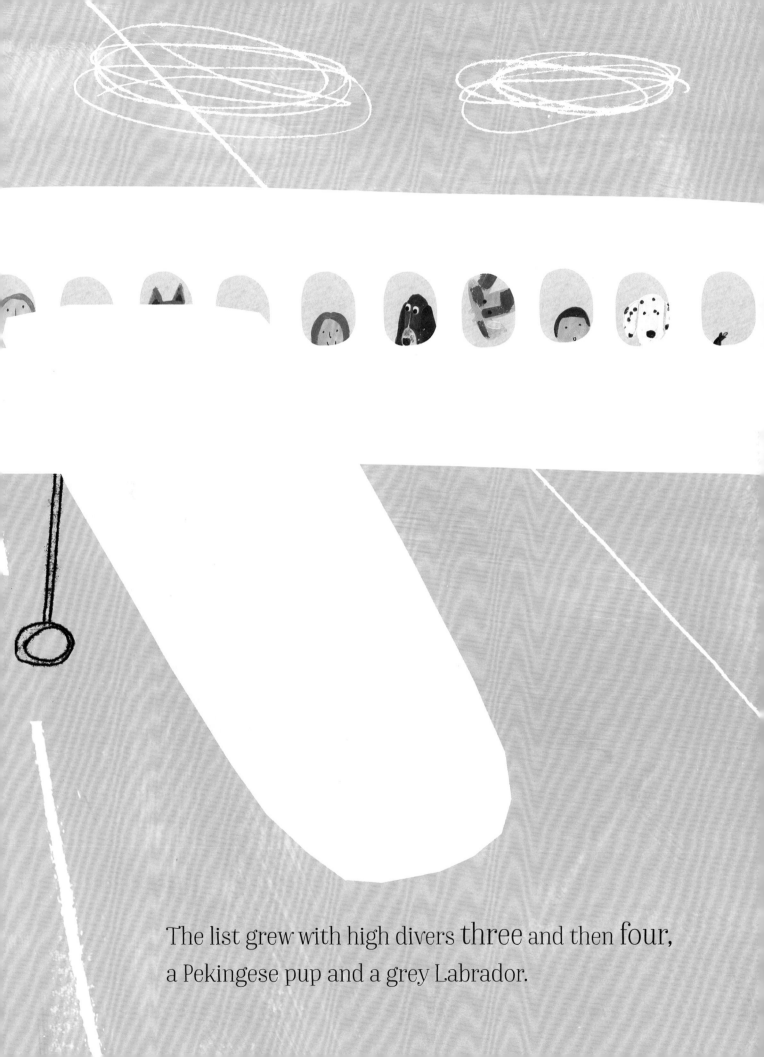

The list grew with high divers three and then four,
a Pekingese pup and a grey Labrador.

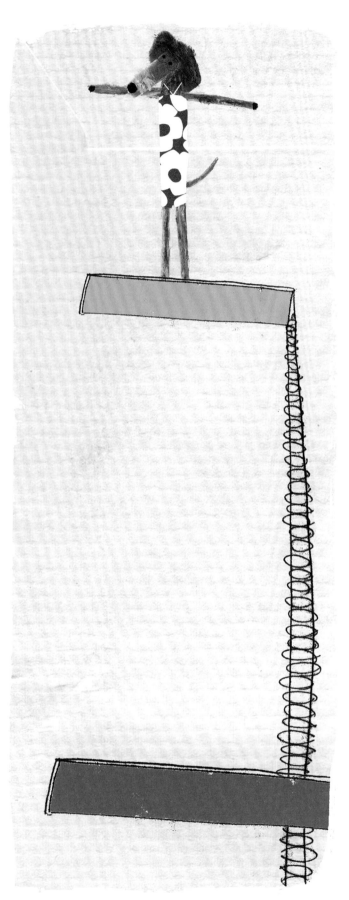

Perrie Piccalilli
was top of the tree,

Terry and Marjorie
as good as can be.

Audrey Armstrong wore a
splendid swim cap,

Derek and Astor
always got a big clap.

Doggy divers lined up
then paraded around,

The competition began
with the
howl
of a hound.

The dogs took turns
soaring down from the top board,

Perrie looped
round and round.

Audrey
flew
like
concord.

It was Bernard's turn next, his tummy in knots,
Our Bassett Hounds' paws were glued to the spot.

His ears flopped down low
and he hid underneath.
He couldn't take part even
gritting his teeth.

Peng Packington
strode from the pool
down below,

Saunders went up
balanced **high**
on tiptoe.

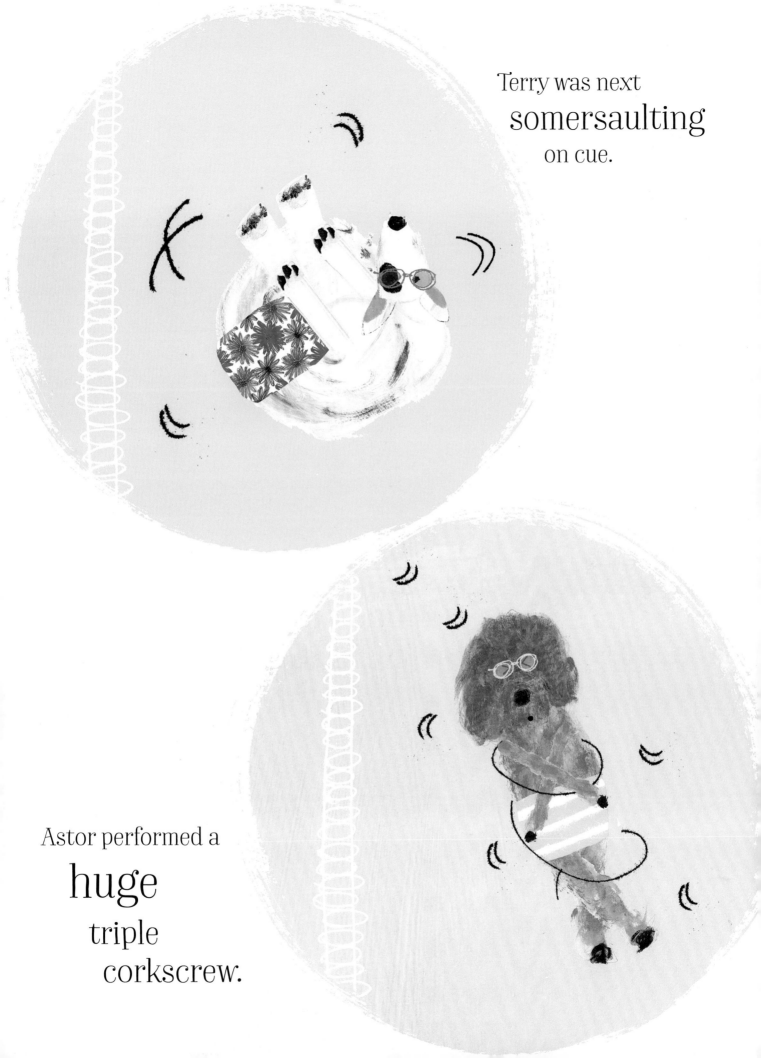

Terry was next
somersaulting
on cue.

Astor performed a
huge
triple
corkscrew.

Bernard, so sad,
started walking away.
Sure that he'd missed
his big break of the day.

But then an announcement
was heard all around,

"It's heat two - come forth if you're a brave diving **hound**".

This had to be it; his last chance for a go,
and Perrie had been watching
(Bernard didn't know).

She'd been really shy once
and knew how it felt.

Seeing Bernard tremble
just made her heart melt.

Holding his paw
Perrie had to insist,

That our talented dog's
chance couldn't be missed.

Before he could back out
he **leapt** off the board,

Somersaulting and spinning
he **spiralled** and **soared.**

Bernard - elated, unclenched his teeth,
Feeling sprightly and agile, and full of relief.

JUDGES

It was one of the **best dives** the judges had seen,
Surely Bernard was so close to reigning supreme.

When all of the dogs finished dive number two,
The judges conferred and the results came through,

Perrie (with most points)
was top of the board,

With Terry and Peng
also up for awards.

Marjorie had achieved
a personal best,

The others enjoying a
well-deserved rest.

The divers came out to the podium stand,

With cheering and clapping (and even a band!)

Overcoming
his shyness
Bernard had
come so far

And was thrilled
when he also
received a
gold star!

So if you find something you really adore,

Don't hesitate; don't make it a chore!

Be brave; take a chance, you just never know,

You might really enjoy it so give it a go!

To my favourite folk – Richard, Edith & Ada.
With HUGE thanks to Jodie, Holly, Ulla, Fay, Maxx & the team at Tate
for all their hard work in helping me make this book come to life.

First published in 2019 by order of the Tate Trustees
by Tate Publishing, a division of Tate Enterprises Ltd,
Millbank, London SW1P 4RG

www.tate.org.uk/publishing

Text and artwork © Lisa Stickley
First published 2019

ISBN 978 1 84976 660 9

Distributed in the United States and Canada by ABRAMS, New York
Library of Congress Control Number applied for
Printed and bound in China by C&C Offset Printing Co., Ltd.
Colour Reproduction by Evergreen Colour Management Ltd.

FSC
www.fsc.org
MIX
Paper from
responsible sources
FSC® C008047